5 m drop 13. 10/98

The Last One In

Strange Matter™
titles in Large-Print Editions:

The Last One In

Marty M. Engle

Gareth Stevens Publishing
MILWAUKEE

For a free color catalog describing Gareth Stevens' list of high-quality books and multimedia programs, call 1-800-542-2595 (USA) or 1-800-461-9120 (Canada). Gareth Stevens Publishing's Fax: (414) 225-0377. See our catalog, too, on the World Wide Web: http://gsinc.com

Library of Congress Cataloging-in-Publication Data

Engle, Marty M.
   The last one in / by Marty M. Engle.
      p.   cm. -- (Strange matter)
   Summary: Thirteen-year-old Michelle, her older sister, and a neighbor boy explore a lakeside cavern searching for a monster which some people think is only a hoax.
   ISBN 0-8368-1671-4 (lib. bdg.)
   [1. Monsters--Fiction. 2. Caves--Fiction. 3. Horror stories.] I. Title. II. Series.
PZ7.E716Las   1996
[Fic]--dc20   96-19606

This edition first published in 1996 by
Gareth Stevens Publishing
1555 North RiverCenter Drive, Suite 201
Milwaukee, Wisconsin 53212 USA

© 1995 by Front Line Art Publishing. Under license from Montage Publications, a division of Front Line Art Publishing, San Diego, CA.

Printed in the United States of America

1 2 3 4 5 6 7 8 9 99 98 97 96

TO OUR FAMILIES
&
FRIENDS
(You know who you are.)

"Hold on, Michelle. Let me give it one more crank," Dad called from the boat.

Easy for him to say. My cut chin plunged below the water again, stinging like crazy. I could barely keep my head above water, even with my yellow life jacket.

"Don't feel too bad, Michelle," Erin called, leaning over the side and trailing her finger in the water. "You did pretty good for your first time up. Just remember to let go of the rope next time."

Erin, my older sister, considers herself a waterskiing expert. Actually, she considers herself an expert on everything. Only fifteen and a red-haired master of the world. She talks a lot but does little.

I am Michelle Boyd. I'm thirteen and my

1

hair is a little lighter than Erin's. I talk a lot and do even less than she does. I swore to myself that would change this summer.

Erin flopped over onto her back and crossed her legs, kicking at the sky. The bright yellow towel she was lying on drooped over the edge of the boat and sloshed against the side.

I didn't feel too bad. My first time water-skiing and I stayed up for almost four minutes. That's pretty good, if I say so myself. Next time I have to remember to let go of the rope. There's nothing like getting dragged on your face across a lake. My nose still ran with water.

"Stupid boat," Dad grumbled, pressing the ignition switch again. The boat had given him a lot of trouble this year. It's really not our boat. It belongs to the Keens next door. They live on Wataga Lake all year. That's gotta be great. We rent a cabin here every summer for a month. The rooms are super big and nice. It's just like a house only better, with real log walls and big screened porches and brick barbecues.

Anyway, the Keens are really nice except for their bratty little blond boy, Billy. He's about ten, though he acts like he's five. They spoil him to death. It's Billy this and Billy that. He gets anything he wants. You should see his room. He has every radio-controlled vehicle known to man; cars and planes, boats and subs, and even a hover craft. It looks like a boat, but has a giant fan on the bottom. It stays about three inches above whatever it's moving over. It is very cool.

Anyway, all he has to do is whine and it's his. Oh, don't get me wrong. He's not all bad. When I broke my leg up here last summer, he hung around with me every day to keep me from getting bored.

It would help if he didn't act so immature. I'm thirteen, so I've outgrown that kind of behavior. But girls mature faster than boys. All girls except Erin. She acts as immature as Billy does. They pick on each other like five-year-olds.

"Got it!" Dad exclaimed. The boat sputtered once, twice, and died.

"Don't get it. Hang in there, sweetie." Dad grabbed the manual. His arms glowed red with sunburn. We had been out on the water most of the day.

"Don't worry about me. I'm not going anywhere," I yelled back. The water was greenish-black, and the coldest I could remember it being. But it felt great. It made me feel alive.

Last summer I wouldn't do anything after I broke my leg jumping off rocks into the lake. I moped around and had zero fun, afraid to do anything. I vowed not to let that happen again.

Nothing would stop me this summer. Sometimes you have to dare yourself to do things you normally wouldn't. I'd always been too scared to waterski before, but here I was. Treading water. Wet as could be. Stayed up four minutes. I couldn't have been happier.

Suddenly Erin pointed across the lake behind me and screamed.

"MICHELLE! LOOK OUT! DAD, GET HER OUT OF THE WATER!" Erin screamed.

Dad dropped the manual and grabbed Erin before she fell out of the boat. They both stared at the water behind me. My heart pounded like a hammer in my chest. My stomach went hollow and knotted tightly.

I turned myself around as quickly as I could. The life jacket made it difficult to move. I scanned the lake desperately, but being at eye level with the water made it almost impossible to see anything.

Then I saw it. A lightning burst of panic froze my body as a wave of nausea churned in my stomach. My head went light. I stopped breathing. My mouth froze in position to scream, but I couldn't make a sound.

Across the lake about two hundred yards away, a greyish-brown hump rose from the water. Sheets of water tumbled down its sides. It plunged back under with a huge splash. It appeared, then disappeared again and again in a serpentine motion. It was HUGE, at least seventy feet.

"GET ME OUT OF HERE! DADDY!" I kicked toward the boat furiously. We were both in the same lake, that thing and me. And I was bite size.

"DADDY! HELP!" I cried, desperately swimming toward the side of the boat.

Dad dove over the side, still fully dressed. I could feel his hands shake as they grabbed my waist. He catapulted me into the boat and quickly climbed back out of the water. I could see the fear in his eyes as he fell to the floor of the boat.

Erin grabbed the video camera and videotaped as best she could. One arm clutched the camera and the other tried to keep her balance on the rocking boat. Her eyes squinched up so tight, I don't know how she saw anything. I tried to control my sobbing as Dad held me tight to his side.

We all watched it now. Not only us, but

6

other boats, too. People pointed excitedly and grabbed cameras.

Something large and alive swam across the lake. We couldn't see a head or neck but it definitely had a hump. It moved up and down in the water very fast and left a V-shaped wake behind it. It moved almost as fast as a ski boat.

"Are you getting it, Erin?" Dad asked breathlessly.

"Oh yeah! It's pretty wild." Erin traced the thing's movements with her camera.

"Use the zoom, Erin. The zoom on the side. The red button," Dad said, moving to her side.

Erin pressed the zoom. "OH MAN!" she cried "Its skin is all brown and wrinkly! I can't believe it! It's gotta be as long as our cabin!"

I looked from Erin across the lake to the moving thing. I couldn't see any detail, but Erin could see lots through the camera. For an instant I thought of snatching the camera myself. I wanted to know what it looked like.

"It's moving up and down real weird. Like it's forcing its way out of the water and then it's like it just lets go and crashes in again." Erin continued to videotape, flapping her arms.

Then she stopped.

"It turned toward us and went under. It disappeared," she said quietly. She looked as if she were afraid to move.

Everyone else on the lake must have had the same reaction. I saw them looking around the lake, as if hoping to catch another glimpse of the mysterious creature.

Suddenly Erin, Dad and I screamed as our boat rose on a swell of water about six feet high! We were all knocked down to the floor of the boat.

Everyone else pointed toward us and yelled, but we couldn't hear what they were saying. A tremendous wall of water had passed under the boat and kept on going.

"It's moving under us!" Dad yelled.

We saw the wave continue past for another minute. Then the water settled, suddenly calm.

Erin tried to hold back tears now. I had already lost it again. I could not accept what had just happened. That thing could have GOT ME! It swam right past where I had been floating minutes before.

"Dad, what was that thing?" Erin asked,

lowering the video camera, her whole body trembling.

"I don't know, sweetie. I don't know." Dad took the camera from her and rewound the tape.

I sat and blinked through stinging tears, wiped my nose and sniffed loudly. "I know. We just saw a lake monster."

I think the entire population of Wataga came to our cabin that evening. Mom and Mrs. Keen turned it into a party. They had snack trays and sandwiches and big fruit platters with watermelon and cantaloupe and strawberries. This is where I planned to hang out most of the night. I could have eaten that whole tray.

Then half a banana hit me smack in the forehead.

I wound up smearing it around more than wiping it off. "Billy Keen, I'm going to kick your butt."

"Got you, monster girl," Billy laughed, crouched at the side of the table. "Or should I say monster lunch! NO! NO! HELP MEEEEEEE!" Billy lowered a grape into his mouth with a giant chomp.

"That's not funny, you little jerk. Grow up." I was in no mood to argue.

"Grow up, Shmo up. If a monster ate you, he'd throw up." He giggled like a lunatic. He could not be stopped when on a hyperactive roll. I chased him into the living room.

The living room ran over with people all talking and waiting to see the video. The people who had been on the lake that day swapped stories about the monster they saw and how it nearly turned our boat over. I wanted to catch the little brat and knock some sense into his head.

Mom stopped me.

"Michelle, quit running through the house and go find Erin. Your father's ready to show the video." Mom placed another tray of cheese and crackers by the lamp in front of the living room window.

What a window. Huge describes it best, ten feet square with a dozen panes. The top of the pine trees in front of the cabin peeked up from below, framing the lake. You could see almost the whole lake from here. From the day bed built into the base of the window, Erin and I would look at it at night. Picture perfect.

"She probably doesn't want to see it again.

She's seen it four times already," I whined.

"Scoot. Now." I couldn't argue with Mom. As usual, she changed my priority. I would check our room first for my missing older sister.

"Come on, Billy, we can go torture her together." I tugged at his sleeve as I stomped toward the hall.

"Torturing you is lots more fun." Billy broke away and ran ahead of me into my room. He slammed the door and locked it, laughing all the while.

I wasted no time. "Dad! Billy's locked himself in my room!" I could see Dad shake his head as he crouched in front of the television. He obviously preferred not to get involved.

Dad slid the videotape in and adjusted the tracking control. He announced to the room that he would show the tape in a few minutes. It turns out that we were the only people to get actual videotape of the thing. The Farners had taken a couple of pictures with their one shot Kodak. An out-of-focus splash in a blurry lake.

"But that splash proves something is alive and swimming around down there!" Mr. Farner exclaimed. "What do you think, Hal? You think the *National Examiner* or one of those TV shows would buy 'em?"

"I don't know, Doug. Maybe. Enough of us saw it. That's for sure," Dad said politely, fiddling with the brightness controls. Dad lived for proper television reception. The picture had to be perfect. He could mess with it for hours.

"Oh hush up, Doug. Ain't nobody gonna want them pictures when they see that video tape. That's hard proof!" George Myer exclaimed.

"And my pictures ain't? Then what are they, Myer?" Doug Farner exclaimed, smacking the arm of his chair and struggling to get up.

"Blurry," George huffed.

"Come on. Settle down," Dad soothed. "They might send up a television crew to interview the whole town!"

That got everyone excited, even me. Then I turned my attention back to my immediate problem, locked out of my *own* room by a spastic little snoop.

"Billy! Open this door now!"

He laughed fiendishly.

"I mean it, Billy."

More laughter. He had his ear pressed to the door on the other side. I could hear the spastic little toad breathing.

"If you don't open this door right now, I'm going straight over to your house, up to your room and I'll pull out all those pictures you have of me in my swimsuit stashed in your dresser."

A sudden silence from the other side of the door and then more hysterical laughter.

I growled angrily and pretended to march down the hall. "I'm as good as there, Billy!" I only made it *sound* like I was marching down the hall. This trick usually works against little snots like Billy.

The door opened a little and I pushed my way in, much to Billy's surprise.

"The only reason I have those pictures is to blackmail you with," Billy sneered.

"Yeah, right." Everything in the room looked intact. Nothing out of place. But no Erin. "Have you seen Erin?"

"Not since this morning." Billy flopped onto Erin's bed.

"This is weird. She's been acting weird all night." I pulled Billy off her bed. "Come on, we better head back. Dad's ready to show the video and he'll be mad if we're not there."

"Okay. Okay. Who cares, anyway? I don't

think it was a monster. I think it was a log."
Billy bounced toward the door.

"Wait a minute. It's a monster! I was right
there. It's some form of animal. Alive, moving
and everything!" No one could make me doubt
what I saw.

"It's a stupid, rotted log," Billy said again
as I grabbed his arm.

Oh, he infuriated me! "How could it have
been a log! It popped out of nowhere and started
swimming. Logs don't do that!"

"A stupid log got unwedged at the bottom
of the lake and popped to the surface. It filled up
with water again and went back under." Billy
yanked loose and ran down the hall back toward
the living room. He didn't believe what he said.
I could tell.

"It's no log," I said under my breath.
Something lives in that lake. Something very
big, very alive, and very, very scary.

I wanted to see it again.

Dad hit the play button. Everyone leaned toward the screen. Billy and I were lying on the floor, right in front of the TV. You could hear a pin drop in the room.

"Here it comes," Dad said as the screen crackled and the lines cleared away.

I felt a familiar knot in my stomach as I watched it play again. There I sat, crying in the boat, with Dad telling Erin to use the zoom. The picture swung around everywhere showing the sky, the shore, the boat, Dad again, and me. I looked scared to death.

"Erin, couldn't you have controlled the camera a little better?" Dad whispered. He looked around but couldn't find her. He looked at me and I shrugged. I didn't know where she'd gone. She could act really flaky sometimes, particularly when it came to family stuff. She always had to be the center of attention.

The camera stopped swinging and refocused on *it*. Big as life. A big brown lump moving rapidly through the water, throwing spray to the sides.

"There you go! See how it's bobbing up and down out of the water. Like it's just under the surface," Dad said.

"It's a log," Billy whispered. I slugged him on the back.

"That thing must have been a hundred feet long!" Mr. Myer cried.

"I'd say it was closer to fifty," Mr. Farner countered with a grunt.

"Seventy by my calculations. Compare its size to the trees on the shore," Dad concluded. "But look how fast it's moving. Had to be at least twenty miles an hour."

"That's about right," Mr. Myer agreed.

The camera zoomed in, and you could see the skin. It took a second for the camera to refocus but then we could see it clearly. It had a large hump and a rough skin texture, like an elephant or . . .

"Bark on a log," Billy whispered. I slugged

him again. "OW! WILL YOU CUT IT OUT!"

"Billy, Michelle. Both of you cut it out," Mom snapped. "Other people are trying to watch."

The camera suddenly lurched straight up and focused on the sky.

"The thing swam under the boat," Dad explained. I shook remembering. It could have swallowed me whole.

The camera swung back down and we saw a big wave moving away from the boat before it settled. Then blackness.

The lights came back on.

"Boy, that's something," Mr. Farner said, stretching. His knees popped as he stood up.

"What are you going to do with the tape, Hal?" Mr. Myer asked.

Dad turned off the VCR. Everyone started to shuffle around and talk excitedly about the possibilities. You could feel the excitement in the room and see the hope on everyone's faces that Lake Wataga would be as big as Loch Ness or Lake Champlain.

"I don't know. I don't know who to send a thing like this to," Dad said.

"Don't you need to send it to the police?"

Mrs. Myer asked.

"No, Harriet. What would they do? Arrest it?" Mr. Myer said sarcastically.

"I already spoke to the sheriff's department," Dad said politely. "They're going to patrol the area for a few days in case it shows up again. To be honest, Sheriff Daley didn't seem overly concerned."

"I know what I'd do. I'd send it to Hard Copy or one of them other TV shows on the unexplained," Mr. Farner said, rubbing his hands together. "They'll probably pay a pretty good chunk of change for something like that."

Doug Farner owned the gift shop by the lake. He had the usual postcards, T-shirts and driftwood junk. I could tell the rusted wheels were turning in his greedy head. "And now it looks like we got ourselves our very own monster. Think what it could mean for tourism."

"Hold on, Doug. I mean we don't really know what it is. It could've been any number of things," Dad said.

"Like what?" Mr. Farner said anxiously.

"Like . . . I don't know. I just don't want to start crying monster yet. That's all. I still want to hear everyone else's opinion."

"Well, I think we got ourselves a legitimate phenomenon. That could mean lots of visitors up here. Now you think about that. I could sell copies of your tape at the gift shop. THE WATAGA LAKE MONSTER! It could be big, Hal. REAL big." Mr. Farner was out of control.

What a tourist-trapping louse! I had nearly been that thing's dinner, and already Mr. Farner wanted to sell monster tickets. Then again, I had the sneaking suspicion that he wasn't the only one.

Mr. Farner and the others didn't understand. Not really. Seeing an unknown animal on a videotape wasn't the same as seeing it live, where it could *get* you. I had watched that weird hump move through the water on the screen, and I also watched it move through the water at *me*.

They didn't know what that was like, feeling their blood run cold, terrified that they were about to pass between giant rows of gnashing teeth into a monster's stomach.

I started shaking and couldn't eat the rest of my watermelon, so I went to the kitchen to throw it away.

Erin stared in the window over the sink. Her face was drawn and as white as a ghost. She appeared terrified. She tapped on the window and signaled me frantically to come outside.

Cold night air blew in off the lake. With the back porch light off, I could barely see through the inky darkness.

"Erin?" I called.

"Over here! Hurry!"

I ran to the side of the house, leaping off the porch stairs. Erin crouched there waiting.

"What are you doing? What's going on? Where have you been? Everyone's been asking about you."

I drew close enough to see her. Erin had this stern look on her face like she knew I'd say no before she said, "We have to go see Mrs. Gloucester."

"WHAT! No way. Dad would kill us. You know how he feels about Old Lady Gloucester."

"You don't understand," Erin said. "I've

been to see her already. You need to talk to her, too. It's about the monster."

"That's where you've been? At that crazy old woman's cabin? You're really asking for it. If Mom and Dad find out, you'll be grounded until you're thirty."

"I told her I'd bring you back with me. They'll never even notice we're gone."

Erin fixed me with pleading, excited eyes. She seemed to have a secret so great that she would die if she didn't tell me.

"Tell me," I said.

"I promised I wouldn't. You have to see for yourself." Erin could barely contain her excitement. It escaped her in nervous giggles. She acted like a five-year-old sometimes.

"You're worse than Billy."

Old Lady Gloucester used to be a doctor or something. Not a medical doctor but something else. She retired to Wataga about thirty years ago, the oldest resident at the lake. She's not very well liked because she's rude to people. She doesn't like anyone on her property and she doesn't like visitors, so everyone leaves her alone.

She's a campfire horror story favorite. I've heard dozens of stories about people who have never returned from her property. Dad says she's a survivalist or something. She won't accept help from anyone. She had a husband, but no one knows what happened to him.

"How did you get past her dog?" I asked. She has this golden retriever named Zu that sounds just like *Zoo*. Zu never lets anyone on the property. Mrs. Gloucester doesn't have visitors. Never.

"You don't understand. We're invited," Erin said with a shudder. She handed me an old torn envelope that had *Erin and Michelle Boyd* scrawled across the middle and Mrs. Gloucester's name scrawled on the back.

I opened it and pulled out the note. It simply said that she needed to speak to us.

"I found it in our mailbox. See? There's no stamp on it. She just came by and shoved it in."

"What does she want? I'm not going over there at this hour. No way."

"Please, Michelle, it won't take long. It's important." Erin wouldn't give up. She'd hound me all night if she had to. She always had to have her way. Once she made up her mind, I could look forward to a night of whining.

"All right. Okay. No more than a half hour. I mean it."

"Let's go. It won't take long. You'll flip out. I promise." Erin tugged me along toward the edge of the lake.

To get to Mrs. Gloucester's, you have to walk around the lake to the end of the cabins where no one had built anything yet. She lives on the only piece of property around the lake that's still pure wilderness.

A very long and winding gravel road led up to her cabin. A steep path through the woods provided a shorter route. Not an easy climb, particularly in the dark.

Suddenly, a tremendous splash erupted from the water beside us.

Water exploded everywhere in giant foamy white sheets! I could see the monster clearly in my mind. It had to be responsible. My heart exploded in my chest.

Erin and I clutched each other and screamed.

The water poured down, drenching our clothes and hair.

I realized that someone had tossed a giant rock into the lake beside us. A perfect toss. Nice distance, good trajectory, perfectly balanced. Obviously not the work of a novice. It had to be a monster of another kind. A bratty kind.

"BILLY!" I cried angrily.

I saw him then, near the bushes, laughing hysterically.

"You little monster," Erin said shaking the water from her hair.

"The only monster around this lake, I'm afraid," Billy said smugly, strolling toward us. "There sure isn't one in the water."

"How can you be so sure, smarty?" I said, wringing the water out of my shirt.

"Because the lake ain't big enough. Where would it hide? What would it eat?"

Erin grabbed Billy before he knew what hit him. "Little bratty boys! That's what he eats!" She twisted his arm behind his back and dragged him to the water. She prepared to toss the little obnoxious jerk in head first.

Billy started to cry before Erin's foot even hit the water. She held him over the dark, lapping water.

"NO! NO! I'M SORRY! ALL RIGHT?! I'M SORRY!" Billy stared down at the water with dread. I had the feeling he was afraid of more than the cold water. His pudgy face twisted into a mask of fright.

"Quit crying, you baby. I'm not gonna toss you in, even though I ought to." Erin dumped Billy on the sand.

"You're going to Old Lady Gloucester's place. That's a pretty stupid thing to do." Billy rubbed his arm as if Erin had broken it.

"What's so stupid about it, nosy?"

"Everybody knows if you sneak onto Old Lady Gloucester's property, she kills you and throws your body in the huge well behind her cabin. The police went up there once to find a

Boy Scout troop that vanished on her property. Know what they found when they got there?"

"What?"

"NOTHING! Because she killed the police and threw them in the well, too! What do you think of that?"

"That's the dumbest thing I've ever heard," I said. "If it's true, how do you know about it?"

"I hear things, man."

Erin and I broke out laughing and ran down the beach toward the empty side of the lake.

There were no cabins and no lights on that side of the lake where the weeds and bushes grew as high as the trees.

On that side of the lake, I knew Mrs. Gloucester sat in the dark on her porch. Watching and waiting.

We sent a pile of rocks bouncing down the hill with our sneakers as we ran. We paused to take a breath at the top of the rise leading to the cabin. I was breathing so hard that I thought I'd bust a lung. We ran almost all the way so we could get back to the house before the party ended, so we wouldn't have to explain where we had been.

The lake looked beautiful from up here in the moonlight. We couldn't help but stop to look at it. The silvery light bounced over the water like a million fireflies all twinkling and shimmering.

"Come on! We have to hurry!" Erin ran ahead of us.

"I have shorter legs. It's not fair," Billy whined.

I punched him on the arm. "Come on. She's right. If Mom and Dad find out where we are, we've had it."

Mrs. Gloucester's cabin wasn't run down or old or decrepit. In fact, it seemed nicer than ours. Bigger anyway, with a satellite dish, a big new deck and a bright green Jeep Cherokee in the garage.

Mrs. Gloucester's husband supposedly left her a lot of money when he died. I should say disappeared. No one knew what had happened to him. He stopped coming into town and a month later he was officially declared a missing person . . . a mystery. A mystery that Mrs. Gloucester wouldn't talk about.

Her dog greeted us first.

A snout full of snarling teeth whirled around the steps at the foot of the deck. A taut chain rattled around its neck as we approached. It was Zu all right.

"I don't think he's in the mood for company," Billy gasped.

"Neither am I," an old, mean voice called from the top of the deck.

We could barely see the shadowy outline of a woman leaning over the redwood railing.

"Mrs. Gloucester?" Erin called. "I brought Michelle . . . and Billy Keen is with us too."

"Not him! Oh very well, be quick about it. It's almost time for the news." The shadowy figure disappeared without a sound through the sliding glass door on the deck.

With a loud click, floodlights popped on everywhere, as if someone had turned on the lights at Disneyworld! They lined the house and garage. Green colored lights lit the rows of trees from below. Two bright spotlights shone on the lake shore far below revealing a little dock with two rowboats.

We started up the deck stairs as Zu retreated under the house in a cowardly fashion. We saw his nose peaking out from the dark. Not a very good guard dog.

We stepped inside and gasped in surprise.

Mrs. Gloucester's living room was a very strange mix of rustic cabin and hi-tech lab. There were VCRs and recording cameras and stereos and large, weird receiver-type devices. She must have known what she was doing as some of them looked in various states of disrepair.

A large telescope jutted out of a window

near the sliding glass door leading to the deck and a huge bookcase stood on the fireplace wall. On a small table by a rear window sat a desk with two large security monitors receiving nothing but static.

Very strange. Why would an old lady have this much electronic stuff?

She closed the door behind us. "Most of this belonged to my husband." She flipped a switch beside the door.

Billy gasped and grabbed my arm as a section of the wall rolled back to reveal a large screen TV.

"It's not often I have celebrities in my house," She said while flipping the channels with a remote she produced from her pocket.

There on the television was a crude digital drawing of a hump in Wataga Lake on a screen behind our local news anchorperson. He commented on reports coming into the station about a monster sighted on the lake that afternoon. He also said that a young girl had a close encounter with the beast. Michelle Boyd.

He said *my* name on the late news along with Dad's and Erin's. Very cool, hearing my name on TV but I didn't like the subject matter.

The television snapped off and the panel slid shut. Mrs. Gloucester nailed us with a terrible stare. "How much do you know about the monster of Wataga Lake?"

"Only that it likes to upset boats and girls," I said quietly. She frightened me almost as much as the lake monster.

"Come over here," Mrs. Gloucester said as she shuffled toward the bookcase. She touched the hair that sat on her head like a nest of white snakes, then she reached for a scrapbook and pulled it down, flipping to a section toward the middle.

She set the book down on a reading table at the foot of the fireplace. Billy, Erin and I huddled around it.

Billy turned the yellowing pages.

We saw a series of news clippings, some dating back to the 1920's. I could not believe it! The stories went on and on. The Wataga Lake Monster used to be a big deal!

Stories of something alive in Lake Wataga went back as far as 1929. They told of mysterious boat accidents on the lake from striking something large and submerged. There were eye-witness accounts and drawings. On and on they went, page after page and year after year. Sightings, recordings, grainy pictures. I saw one picture that looked almost exactly like what I'd seen in the lake that afternoon. A big brown hump moving through the water.

Then nothing but blank pages.

The clippings ended in the fifties. Strangely enough, after 1955 the monster disappeared and the stories died.

"I don't get it. All this time, a monster lived in the lake and everybody just forgot?" I asked. Mrs. Gloucester didn't seem the type to like to answer a lot of questions but she'd kept this book. She had to have *some* answers.

Mrs. Gloucester sneered at me, her eyes narrow and vicious. "You know very little about this lake. About its secrets."

She moved uncomfortably close to me. Her gaze never moved from mine. Nervous fear kept me planted where I stood. She didn't smell very good, especially when her nose hovered inches from mine.

"You have, no doubt, heard of my husband?" she asked.

I shook my head. This seemed to infuriate her, as if everyone should know her husband.

"Harold P. Gloucester, the renowned biologist and cryptozoologist? You have never heard of him? Impossible! Do you even know what a cryptozoologist is?"

"No." I couldn't pull my eyes away from hers. Her low monotone held me in a trance.

"A cryptozoologist is a person who looks for animals that may or may not exist."

"L-Like the monster in the lake," I stammered.

"The monster is why Harold and I moved here." Mrs. Gloucester's smile looked phony.

"You see, Harold came here often as a young boy with his father, to fish and to camp. His father told him stories of the monster, but Harold never believed them. That is, until he saw the monster at age twelve when it tipped their fishing boat over. Much like your incident today." She pointed a bony finger at me and smiled.

"His father drowned."

Shocked, I backed into Erin and Billy, who stood behind me, looking equally horrified.

Mrs. Gloucester closed her eyes and, with each passing moment, her voice grew sadder and more intense.

"With one fatal pass, the monster had changed Harold's life forever. The authorities found nothing when they dragged the lake.

"Only Harold's father.

"In the end, they ruled it a simple boating accident. No one, of course, believed the twelve-year-old Harold."

Mrs. Gloucester lurched at us suddenly, her eyes wide. Her hands trembled.

"By age thirty, he had became obsessed, crazed! He staked his professional reputation on finding the monster. His friends and colleagues laughed at him for living in such a remote area, looking for something that simply didn't exist.

"For twenty-nine years he searched. Despite his best efforts, he failed. He found nothing in that cold, dark lake but muddy water.

"Nothing that even hinted at the existence of a monster.

"He died a broken man in 1955.

"Stories of the monster faded. People forgot. Many years later, cabins sprang up, the wonderful tourist industry started, and people like your parents moved in.

"The monster ceased to exist."

Mrs. Gloucester walked to the window

and stared down at the lake.

My anger swelled. "I don't understand. What about all the sightings? Tons of people saw it! I saw it myself this afternoon. I hadn't imagined it. Something lives in the lake. It almost got me!"

I felt tears stinging in my eyes.

"Why would it just stop showing up after your husband *died*? Why did it choose to come back now?!" I yelled.

"There's a very good reason it stopped showing up after my husband died."

Mrs. Gloucester glared at me. My heart skipped a beat.

"Did you tell them?" she asked Erin.

"No. Not yet."

"Take them out back and show them."

"Show us what?" I felt the hair standing up on the back of my neck as Erin signalled for us to follow her.

If I had known what she was about to show us I would have *run* all the way back home.

We walked in single file through the kitchen, out another glass door, down some stairs to a big grassy backyard, dark and foreboding with storm clouds churning overhead.

Storms hit often and suddenly at the lake. It was best to be indoors, not out in a backyard and definitely

. . . not staring at a well.

Billy was right. There was a well almost as big as a pool and wide enough to hide an army. . . or at least a Boy Scout troop and several policemen.

From across the yard, we couldn't see how deep the well went.

"What are you showing us, Erin?" I asked. I didn't like this at all, and I especially didn't like the look on Erin's face. As if she had a wonderful but dreadful secret to reveal.

Without a word, she bolted to the side of the porch and slipped under a blue canvas tarp covering a wood pile and something else . . . something large.

Suddenly a loud hissing sound came from the well.

"What's that noise?" Billy asked.

I didn't answer. That deep, dark well had me transfixed.

Something had started to fill it. My heart pounded faster. My eyes widened with terror.

A large brown hump rose from the well with a disgusting hissing noise. It pulsated in the dim light filtering through the trees.

My knees went weak. IT WAS ALIVE! I relived every terrifying moment on the lake that day, the nausea, the paralysis. For a moment I wondered what it would be like to be in a monster's stomach. I imagined the jaws closing around me as I saw the Wataga Lake Monster rise out of a well in Gloucester's backyard.

It lunged forward out of the well and came straight for us, swallowing us whole.

9

The sound of Erin's laughter brought us back to reality.

We kicked and screamed at the big brown lump that had draped over us and started rapidly. . . deflating.

"It's just a stupid balloon!" Billy yelled.

"I can see that, you moron!" I retorted.

Erin had a good laugh watching us kick and squirm our way out from under all that brown rubber. It stank something awful, like thirty years of mold and mildew.

"BE CAREFUL YOU DON'T DAMAGE THE MOTOR!" Mrs. Gloucester called from the back porch. She held her back as if she were in pain, seating herself on the steps.

"Oh man, that was priceless." Erin laughed until she couldn't draw a breath.

I crawled out from under the brown rubbery thing a much unhappier but wiser person, not to mention furious. I blew the hair out of my face and marched up to Erin to smack her.

"Hey! Cut it out, dweeb." She kept on laughing.

"Not funny, Erin. Not funny at all." Billy's lips quivered, slurring his words.

"Isn't it cool, though?" Erin pointed behind me.

We turned to look at it. It had mostly deflated now and draped itself halfway out of the well. It was about fifty feet long and shaped like a football with a long neck and a long tail. Four inflatable flippers poked from the sides and toward the center, a small square bulge poked through, revealing itself to be a motor.

"It's remote controlled, I'll bet, like my submarine," Billy concluded. He stared at the motor intently.

"Very good, young man. It *is* remote controlled. My husband added that feature just before he died." Mrs. Gloucester pointed at Erin who revealed the control unit under the tarp. It did look like the controls to one of Billy's toys.

"Call it the last desperate attempt for a

man to save his reputation. He figured if he couldn't find a real monster, he'd build one. At least to keep the stories going so he could make a hasty retreat.

"Of course he never truly retreated.

"He believed to the very end that *something* dwelled in that lake somewhere,
. . . and if he just hung in there long enough, he'd find it."

"So when he died, the monster *did* stop roaming the lake. He wasn't around to control it." I kicked at the rubber thing with disgust.

I felt like the butt of the biggest practical joke of all time.

"So why today? Why did you make it attack our boat?"

As Mrs. Gloucester rose, her back gave a loud pop and she winced. "I take it out on the lake every now and then . . . just to keep it running. It had been a long time. The controls went out and it took me awhile to get them to work again. Running into you was an accident. I always keep it up here near my dock if I can, out of sight."

"Man. The Wataga Lake Monster is a hoax after all," Erin said. "She sure had us fooled."

I wasn't laughing. I didn't think it was funny at all. "Why'd you tell us? Why didn't you keep it a secret?" My anger grew by the second.

Mrs. Gloucester took one last harsh look at us before vanishing back into her gloomy abode. Though we couldn't see her in the shadows of her home, we could hear her low voice.

"The last thing I want or need is a lake full of curious, sloppy tourists crowding every dock and swarming over every patch of sand, polluting the lake with their cameras, their garbage, and their foul presence, searching for something that is not there. What happened today was a mistake. Nothing more. A grim little reminder of the waste my husband made of his life. It will not happen again. . . I have decided to destroy it."

Billy looked crushed at the thought of the ultimate in remote controlled toys being totally obliterated.

"That still doesn't answer my question." I stared up at the shadowy doorway. "Why'd you tell us?"

"Maybe I showed you so you wouldn't spread the stories anymore. Let them die like they did before."

Her voice began to trail off.

"Or maybe I showed you so someone would know. You decide."

For a moment, a dead silence hung in the thin mountain air.

"There is no lake monster," Billy whispered happily. He and Erin laughed.

I couldn't be sure. Had Mrs. Gloucester told us the whole truth?

In only a little while, Billy wouldn't be so sure either.

10

"I told you! There is no monster! Billy called for the hundredth time. I didn't look up from the dark, rocky path to acknowledge him this time. What a creep.

Erin yelled at him for me. "Will you shut up!" She slung a small rock at him and nailed him square in the forehead. Not unusual. That's why she's always the pitcher on our camp softball team.

"Ow! That could have put my eye out!"

"I was aiming for your MOUTH!" Erin snapped.

I wanted to turn and let him have it. Unfortunately, he was smart enough to stay out of range. He badgered me all the way down the path. Calling me stupid for believing in a lake monster. Saying I needed glasses.

Before I could punch him out, I noticed a mist crawling through the woods.

The cabin had vanished from sight. All we could see were the skeletal trees and the shrouded lake. A faint mist crawled across the lake surface like a billowy white blanket. I hadn't seen a night like this on the lake in a long, long time. I knew the mist would continue to gather until we couldn't see four feet in front of us.

"Let's hurry. It's getting late, and they'll start to check on us soon. Farner can't keep Dad busy blabbing all night."

An uneasy feeling swept over me. Small wonder, between the talk about lake monsters and weird, old Mrs. Gloucester. I had a feeling that something terrible was about to happen.

Sometimes a dare can be a little more than a dare. Sometimes a dare is a challenge you make to yourself, to push yourself a little further than you normally would go, just to see what stupidity you really are capable of.

Sometimes, if the time is right and the wrong people are around, a dare can send a person into an incredibly idiotic and dangerous situation. A situation that could get worse by the minute.

I thought about this on the shore of the mist shrouded lake at the bottom of the hill after I dared Billy to put up or shut up.

We stood on the dock with the two row boats. The spotlights that had lit the brackish water before remained dark and silent now. No electric hum. Only the sound of gently lapping water against the wooden barrels keeping the dock afloat. I glared through the mist on the shore at the small boy in a defiant posture.

"Well?" I asked again.

Silence.

"Come on Billy. Mr. Sure-of-Himself," I sneered. I had him and he knew it.

He stood there in silence. He had painted himself into a corner. I watched as he licked his lips feverishly and his knees began to quake. He seemed dizzy and light-headed. His legs looked weak and wobbly.

Erin said nothing, amazed at the challenge issued to my tormentor.

If he didn't do what I dared him to, he'd be admitting the nagging doubt in his head about the existence of the monster.

"ALL RIGHT! ALL RIGHT! I'll do it." Billy caved in. His mental defenses must have given way. It happens to everyone I guess, whenever you set yourself up as the expert and someone calls you on it.

"But only in a boat," he said.

"OH NO! You have to swim! Swim a hundred feet out and back or you can shut up about it the rest of your unnatural, annoying life," I countered quickly.

No question about it, a boat would add an element of security. For Billy to prove his point, he would have to brave the lake alone. Swim one hundred feet out into the blackness and back. No protection. Nothing.

Billy's face twisted into a tight little ball of anger as he stormed to the end of the dock, pulling off his shoes as he went. He threw his shirt onto the dock. Only his denim shorts remained, cut off by his mother after he'd worn the knees out spying on Erin and me.

He had built up great momentum, a little steam train, a bulldozer that no doubt or fear could stop.

Erin and I stood and watched in utter amazement as a pink fleshy shape dove off the end of the boat dock, through the swirling mist and into the dark, mysterious waters of Wataga Lake.

Followed promptly by an ear-splitting, blood-curdling scream.

11

"THIS WATER IS FREEZING!" Billy's cry must have carried for miles across the lake. Owls swooped from the trees and I pictured wild deer running from the pitiful cry that echoed through the woods.

Erin and I ran to the dock, steadying ourselves at the edge as the barrels bobbed under our weight. We looked down and saw Billy's head poking out of the blackness. He gritted his teeth and clutched himself tightly. Every hair on his body must have been standing straight up in the freezing cold.

"I hope you're s-s-satisfied," Billy chattered as he paddled around to face us.

"Not yet. Start swimming. A hundred feet at least."

Billy dog paddled away from the dock into

the inky blackness. We could barely see his head through the mist.

When he got about twenty feet out he turned his head. We could barely see him.

"Far enough?" He spit water out of his mouth. His arms flailed around him.

"No way. Keep going." Erin sounded as if she enjoyed this. Next to softball and cheese-burgers, torturing Billy was her favorite sum-mer pastime.

Usually he deserved it and normally I went along, but this time was different. This time I let Billy's nagging get to me and lashed back. And I'd gone too far.

I'd dared him to swim a hundred feet in a dark lake to prove he didn't believe in the mon-ster. Erin hadn't dared him. I did.

My senses returned. He could be in real danger over a stupid dare.

What had I done?

An overwhelming dread swept over me. Billy's badgering had fogged my brain but now I could think clearly. I knew that Billy had to get out of the water, and he had to do it now!

"Billy! That's far enough!" I cried with my hands cupped to my mouth. "COME BACK!

RIGHT NOW! I MEAN IT!"

"Hey. What are you doing?" Erin said, annoyed. "Forget it, Billy! KEEP GOING!"

"NO! Billy, come in here. Come in here right now! Please!" I could hear something now. Something moved in the water. Something big.

"You're as bad as he is." Erin clamped her hand over my mouth. "KEEP GOING, BILLY! OR YOU'LL NEVER, EVER HEAR THE END OF IT!"

I could barely see him. I guessed how he felt because I had done the same thing that very afternoon. Treading water, watching it wash and splash against his chin as he floated neck deep, the same as I had done.

A splash erupted from the water.

Not from Billy. He had stopped moving the moment it happened.

Another splash. Louder. Closer. No other noise on the entire lake. The mist blew in puffs across his face. He spit out another mouthful of lake water.

"Erin? Michelle? You guys still there?"

"Shut up Billy. We hear something." Erin's voice lowered.

"I-I-I'm. I-I'm going to come in now. You

guys can make fun of me all you want."

Billy moved forward in the water but stopped as he heard another splash.

"OH! Did you see that? DID YOU SEE THAT!" Erin pointed to the right. I looked where she was pointing. Nothing.

"I saw something! Right over there. I swear. Billy! You better come in now!" Erin yelled. She sounded as panicky as I felt.

Billy lunged forward now in big splashing strokes. He moved as if he was swimming through syrup. We could tell in his panic, he would never make it back to the dock on his own. My heart sank as my stomach hollowed.

Then the wave came.

The water swelled beneath him. Billy's body rose in the water with the wave.

We saw his tiny head suddenly rise up twelve feet in the air, poking out of a giant black hill of water. An enormous wave held him suspended.

Like the wave today when we were water skiing! Just like . . .

"Oh man, SOMETHING IS MOVING UNDERNEATH HIM!" I yanked my shoes off and dove into the water, while Erin stood screaming hysterically.

Billy bounced on top of the monster wave that had him. I saw a dark shadow in the wave, even darker than the water, shaped like a whale or a shark. I couldn't be sure because the water distorted the image so much.

Something definitely moved beneath him, gliding effortlessly through the water.

Scared out of my mind, I swam toward him. I watched this huge, unending shadow pass right under him, and could only hope it wouldn't turn on me. I had to reach Billy. I had to help him.

"I TOUCHED IT WITH MY FOOT!" Billy screamed as the wave passed beneath him. He tossed around as if he were in a wild panic, unable to swim.

The mist blew back in.

I swam as fast as I could toward him. My face would hit the water hard and I'd roll to the side to grab a big lungful of air before I hit the water again. If I couldn't reach Billy fast, he'd be a goner.

"Billy! Hang on!"

I saw his head still poking out of the water, sobbing in great gulping gasps. About twenty feet behind him, another wave, headed straight for him . . . and me. I swam furiously, determined to get to him before the wave hit.

Behind me, I heard Erin scream something about a boat. I didn't have time to turn.

I reached Billy.

He grabbed my neck in a panic, nearly choking me. We were both floundering as the wave steadily moved behind us.

Then Billy must have passed out. He went limp and slid under the water.

"BILLY!" I screamed and clutched at his sinking body, struggling to keep us both afloat.

Then a strange quiet settled over the water. Like a lull in a storm or the center of a hurricane. The mist drifted.

I looked to one side.

A large brown hump cut through the water right beside me! Not rubber, not something that had been inflated, but *alive* and moving beside me like a large brown wall! It rose ten feet high and sheets of water washed off its back. It moved with amazing speed.

I was right beside it. White flashes of terror froze my blood. With horror, I watched as my hand reached out. Then, the unthinkable.

I touched it.

My fingers glided across the sandpaper surface of the skin as the creature passed. The tips of my fingers stung and bled but I held my hand there until the wall of brown had passed.

My mind shut down. I couldn't think. I couldn't hear anything but my own rapidly beating heart and the rush of wind in my head. Tears filled my eyes and a scream raced up my tightened throat.

I turned my head slowly to watch the hump cut through the mist toward the dock!
I watched as Erin froze in her boat, the knotted rope lashing it to the dock, still in her hands.

She would have come after us in the boat, if she had managed to untie it.

The hump submerged and plowed into the dock. My whole body tightened with dreadful anticipation.

Barrels and wooden debris flew through the air like a cyclone had hit.

Erin landed in the water and swam toward the sandy shore.

The hump disappeared.

I finally dragged Billy to shore and cried my eyes out as Erin helped me to my feet.

Safe. Safe on land. Away from the *thing*. Billy came to, confused and scared to death. He collapsed on the sand in an exhausted heap.

"I thought . . . I thought it . . ." Erin choked the words out, reaching for me.

"I thought so, too," I sobbed and hugged Erin as hard as I could.

Billy shot up from the sand with his eyes wide. His finger thrust out in front of him. His mouth stretched to a perfect circle.

"LOOK!" he cried.

Erin and I turned and saw a brown wrinkled hump about a hundred feet out. It had stopped moving.

A graceful neck unfurled from under the hump and rose into the air. It looked like a swan's neck, a gentle 'S' curve, dripping with water. On top of that neck, a head emerged.

A snake's head.

It turned and looked straight at the shore. Straight at us. Then it slowly sank and disappeared.

We were all speechless.

I looked away from the spot and noticed my hand. I stared at my bloody fingers and realized I had proof.

Not like Dad's tape or the blurry photographs in a scrapbook, but proof nonetheless. Proof to myself that it was real.

The sky was bright blue and sunny. It almost hurt your eyes to look at it. We had snuck home just in time last night. We told Mom and Dad that we'd been at the Keens' with Billy, and since the Keens were at our place, they didn't know the difference.

Dad closed the front door behind us as we ran toward the study with our arms full of books. Billy ran ahead as usual.

"Don't run with your arms full!" Mom called from the kitchen as we zipped past.

Billy closed the door to the study as we set the piles of books on the reading table. "Monsters of the Sea" by Richard Ellis and "The Monster of Loch Ness" and "Sea Serpents of the Past and Present." We had about twenty books. It would take us awhile to get through them all, but serious research would be the key to this mystery.

Billy snapped the large blinds shut in the huge picture window, blocking out the lake, the mountains and the sun.

Erin turned on the overhead lights. They looked like oil lamps but had a flame-shaped lightbulb in them. They had a dimmer and Erin turned them down low.

I opened the first book and we gathered around to read.

For what we were planning, we needed to know everything we could about lake monsters.

Mrs. Gloucester had obviously not told us everything. That rubber thing in her well was not the only monster in Lake Wataga.

Billy and I had the scabs to prove it.

The blurry, fuzzy image looked more like a xerox than a photograph. It showed the calm surface of a lake and a mysterious black shape that looked like a swan coming out of the water. A silhouette, it looked amazingly like what we'd seen last night.

"That's it. I'm telling you that is what we saw." I was so excited I could hardly sit still.

"That's the most famous picture of the Loch Ness Monster ever taken. Didn't you hear? It's a fake," Billy said. "Some doctor and a big-game hunter got together, carved this head out of wood and attached it to the top of a tin toy submarine. It made the news everywhere. The guy who helped carve it confessed before he died of old age. They heard someone coming and stepped on it in the water. They sank it in the shallow bay where they photographed it."

"But nobody's ever found it. At least not yet," Erin concluded.

Ever since last night, she had taken on a different attitude. She'd treated it like an exciting joke before. Now she took it seriously. She had been a lot nicer to Billy, too.

"That's my point. Nobody's ever found it. The guy could have been lying," I insisted.

"Oh come on. Why would he lie about making it up?" Billy asked. He turned the page. "Look at all this stuff. That monster could be anything in any one of these books."

"Okay. But what about all the other sightings at Loch Ness? People have been seeing it since the sixth century." I would not give up on my favorite theory.

According to the books, Loch Ness has been *the* hot spot of cryptozoologists since the thirties when in 1934 Dr. Kenneth Wilson took the picture we were arguing about before. I had heard of the Loch Ness Monster like everybody else but I had no idea of the history *behind* the monster.

"For example, in the sixth century St. Columba heard that a monster had attacked and killed a swimmer at Loch Ness. When he went there, he sent a swimmer of his own across the lake to bring back a boat on the other side.

"The monster heard the swimmer and roared up on him with his mouth wide open. St. Columba told the monster not to attack the man and to swim away. The monster did, and no one saw it again until the thirties.

"Since then there have been hundreds of people looking for the monster. They have used minisubs and underwater cameras. Sonar. Radar. They even sent in two dolphins with cameras strapped to their backs to look for it.

"In 1975, the Rhines expedition took underwater pictures with super bright strobe lights. Most were too blurry to see, but one of them showed what could have been a diamond shaped flipper. Still, no one has come up with a clear picture of the thing underwater," I read aloud.

"You'd think with all this equipment and all these scientists, they would be able to get a good picture of it," Billy muttered.

"The problem is the water is full of algae-like stuff called *peat*. It floats in the water and makes it a mucky brown. A few feet down and you can't see more than two yards in any direction. Must be like our lake."

Billy strained to read over my shoulder. I continued. "Still, there have been a few good pictures and even a *movie* of the monster taken by Tim Dinsdale in 1960. It showed something moving through the water very fast, leaving a 'V' shaped wake behind it. It definitely showed a live object, according to the Royal Air Force who analyzed the film.

"On top of that there were hundreds and hundreds of eye witnesses who have seen the monster in the water and on land, like Mr. and Mrs. George Spicer who watched a large humped-back thing move across the road in front of them while they were near the Lake one night in 1934." I turned the page.

"Okay, Michelle. You're right. Just because one picture turned out to be a fake, it doesn't mean the monster's a fake. But what do these scientists think the Loch Ness Monster is?" Billy asked.

"Some think it's a seal or an otter. Some think it's a giant fish or even a worm."

"What we saw last night was not a seal or an otter or a fish or a worm," Erin said.

We read about dozens of other lake and sea monsters from all over the world. Like "Champ" who lives in Lake Champlain and according to eye witness reports looks amazingly like its cousin in Loch Ness. Or the sea serpent who haunted the shores of Massachussets in 1817, sighted by over a hundred people during the summer. The list went on and on and on.

We decided after poring through every book on the subject, that we had a monster who didn't match any of them.

Then Erin found it in a book on dinosaurs.

14

It looked so much like our monster, I immediately grabbed the book out of Erin's hands to get a closer look. The creature in the picture had a longer neck. Its head was smaller and it wasn't as muscular as our monster, but otherwise they matched.

"Nothing that a hundred million years of evolution couldn't fix," Billy quipped.

We stared at the picture, labeled *"Plesiosaur,"* a nasty-looking reptile that ruled the oceans in the Mesozoic Era. Large, sharp teeth in a small head with a long neck and a big humped back. Big flippers and a stubby tail. Almost like our monster, but a little different.

"This thing lived in the ocean. Salt water. This is a freshwater lake," Erin noted.

"Well, Lake Wataga was probably connected to the ocean a hundred million years ago. This guy's probably some kind of freshwater relative that got cut off. It's definitely smaller and probably stronger," Billy said.

"If that's true, then it's a reptile. That means it has lungs, not gills, and breathes air, not water. It has to come up for breath just like a lizard or an alligator," I said.

"Yeah. So?" Billy had started to pace around the room. I could tell he was excited. I could practically see the wheels turning in his head.

"Well, this lake isn't *that* big. If it had to breathe air and come up all the time, people would have been seeing it a lot more often than they have in the last forty years," Erin said.

I broke in, closing the book. "Unless it had someplace to hide. Someplace where it could breathe without being seen."

"Yeah, but how could it have stayed hidden since 1955? It hasn't been seen since her husband died. That's a long time to stay under, even if it *did* have a secret place to hide in," Erin said.

"It must have! You saw it yourself last night! It practically swallowed us!" Billy

67

exclaimed, rubbing his arms.

"True. And that thing found *us* pretty easily. I can't believe that her hot-shot biologist husband never found a thing. He *must* have seen it. So why would he build a fake monster?" Erin asked.

Then I spied the wooden duck that Dad kept on the fireplace.

An idea hit me.

"I think I know why he built a fake monster. And I think I know where to start looking."

Erin and Billy looked at me with surprise.

They seemed to be shocked that I actually wanted to go looking for it, and I must admit, I surprised myself.

I swore I would be a doer this summer and crazy or not, I had to know the truth about the monster.

"Get the camera. We're going to take the next great monster photograph. And it won't be a hoax," I said as I closed the book.

As we approached the lake, we saw the first news crews. They had large dish antennas and big splashy channel numbers on the sides of their vans.

Men and women were checking their microphones in the picnic area by the shore. Then we saw the buses and minivans and cars. We wound our way through a maze of jammed-together vehicles.

Someone in a red pickup honked at us as we tried to make our way across the public parking lot toward the lake. I didn't see a single empty parking spot among the hundreds of cars there.

Families. Tourists. Reporters. You couldn't see the beach for the people. No room to move or walk or sit down. Every square inch of the shore was covered by people.

People had pitched tents in every available spot. Fires from weenie roasts filled the air with smoke. Cans floated in the water. Beach balls bounced through the air.

Despite the crowd, finding a place to swim was no problem. No one was in the water. There were people having picnics, but very few people chose to swim.

Boating was another story.

Motor boats, pontoon boats, rowboats, sailboats. All were cruising the crowded lake.

Boats smacked into other boats as rapidly as cars in the parking lot smacked into other cars. Moms smacked their noisy kids. Photographers smacked their cameras and one fat guy smacked the static-filled screen of the TV set in the bed of his pickup.

All these people were here for one thing and one thing only, to get a glimpse of the beast. The monster of Wataga Lake.

"The monster of Wataga Lake! Own the tape that made him famous! Only $10.00 a copy! See it before everyone else does on the news tomorrow night!" Doug Farner cried from his mobile souvenir stand.

Oh no. He had already talked Dad into selling copies of our video tape. And, man, were they selling! He had T-shirts and post cards and bumper stickers that said "I love the Wataga Lake Monster." People crowded the stand so heavily we could hardly see it.

"This sucks," I said.

"I can't believe this. Overnight," Erin agreed.

"I want a T-shirt." Billy attempted to work his way through the crowd.

"Oh no you don't. Come on." Erin grabbed him by the collar and dragged him along.

We had a better place to go. It was just behind and under Mr. Myer's lakeside restaurant, "The Hungry Bear", with the carved wooden bear out front.

The line for the restaurant stretched out the door and into the street. A very happy Mr. Myer stood on the porch. A lot of grumpy people stood in line.

"The best darn burgers and barbecue you ever will eat," Mr. Myer told them.

We even saw a few kids from school. Darren and David Donaldson waited at the end of the line, fighting with their parents, as usual, and just a little way ahead of them was Curtis Miller! I think Curtis is the greatest. He never pays attention to me, though.

A very steep embankment could be found behind the restaurant that led to the lake. A very unattractive area with no real beach, only rocks and mud and mosquitos and little in the way of scenery.

However, it had something of interest to almost every kid who'd ever lived on the lake.

A hole.

A very, very deep hole.

It was the kind of hole you were compelled to drop something into. And the kind of hole where you never hear anything hit bottom. Every kid on the lake had looked at the hole or played around it at least once. It became known as "The Hole".

"Some kids I heard of even tried going down in The Hole, once," Billy said soberly as he stared down into the inky blackness. "But they always chickened out. Or were never heard from again."

"You hear everything, Billy," I groaned as I peered into the inky blackness.

"It's more of a crevice," Erin corrected.

"You guys are nuts. Are you sure you want to do this?" Billy asked.

"We have to know for sure," I said.

Billy asked the dreaded question. "Well, who's going to go first?" We had not brought it up for fear of getting the job ourselves. Now it had to be decided.

We all stared at this small, overgrown crevice in the rocks and then looked over the lake that stretched to Mrs. Gloucester's wilderness on the other side.

The lake laughed at us. Taunted us. Dared us to go into The Hole.

One week earlier, Skinny Joe Alister went around the lake telling everyone he'd heard a terrible cry come out of The Hole. He and his even skinnier little brother were throwing rocks in when they heard it.

He said it was the most horrible, unearthly cry imaginable. It sounded like it came from miles under the earth.

He got so scared, he ran off and left his little brother crying there. His mother rounded them both up and they haven't seen daylight since.

No one paid attention.

No one believed him.

We believed him now.

"I'll go first." I heard myself saying it, though I couldn't believe it.

As I said before, sometimes you have to dare yourself. If we were right we'd have a picture that would go right next to the doctor's picture of the Loch Ness Monster in that book.

If we were wrong. . . well, at least we could say we solved the mystery of The Hole.

"Flashlight."

"Check." Billy handed me the flashlight.

"Rope."

"Check." Erin double-checked the rope looped around my waist and tied it around a support beam on the back of the restaurant.

"Matches. Check." I felt in my pocket for my waterproof matches. Dad said to always carry them when we're at the lake because "you never know". I still didn't know what he meant.

"Camera."

"Check." Erin handed me the one you just point and click, with a built-in flash.

"Talk me out of this. Please?" I said.

No response.

"Well, lower me in then."

They lowered me into The Hole feet first as I took a last look at the surface of the lake beside me. Billy looked at me with just my head sticking out of the blackness.

"Good luck," they both said. I felt the sunlight on my face disappear, followed by a cool darkness.

16

The blackness in front of my eyes was peaceful and quiet.

I turned on my flashlight.

The beam immediately hit the rocks on all sides of the very cold, very nasty and very cramped space. I twisted and turned on the end of my rope.

"Okay! Lower away!" I called.

With a jerk and a tug, I started my descent. Bits of dirt and mud fell below me as they scraped against my sides.

I aimed my flashlight straight down to see how far the mud fell, but the dark swallowed the beam. This was worse than I thought it would be. Already I could feel the walls closing in as the opening grew smaller above. I felt hot and flushed even though the temperature continued to drop and chill bumps grew on my legs and arms.

What little light filtered in from above soon vanished. Alone in a tight muddy tube with a single flashlight beam to light my way down, I could see spiders crawling on the sides of the walls and earthworms that curled around twisted roots I never dreamed of seeing.

"This is really gross you guys. I just WANT YOU TO KNOW!" My voice echoed around me as I continued to descend.

At this point, the opening of the passage grew wider and I could swing around a bit. I flashed my light in all directions so nothing could get the drop on me. Everywhere it hit revealed something slimy, muddy or gross. I felt sick to my stomach and every hair on the back of my neck bristled.

Lower and lower I dropped until the rope started to jerk and twitch, lowering me harder and rougher.

"Hey! Watch it up there!" I yelled, shining my light straight up into blackness.

No response.

I continued my descent.

The Hole widened until I could barely

touch both sides of it at the same time. Shelves of rock and small crevices lined the walls here. I saw the first formations of stalactites jutting inside some of the crevices. In the distance I heard the faint sound of running water.

I had room to swing. Back and forth. Back and forth. Against one wall and then the other. One wall and then the other. Then I hit the wall and felt something long and slimy drop into my hair.

I SCREAMED and started kicking and yelling.

"SOMETHING'S IN MY HAIR!" I reached up and grabbed what felt like a snake! I pulled at it as it slithered down my back.

I kicked and tossed and flailed about so hard I didn't notice what I was doing to the rope. I didn't hear the creaking or the cries of Erin and Billy telling me to hold still.

I *did* feel the jolt of the rope breaking.

It felt like I fell forever before I hit the rocky bottom of the crevice and tumbled into the cave. At least, the echo made it sound like a cave.

I couldn't see anything.

The fall had broken my flashlight.

17

I didn't waste any time. Nothing was broken except the flashlight. I had some scrapes and scratches, but no permanent damage. I grabbed the thing out of my hair. It turned out to be a root.

I sat, terrified, in the complete and total darkness of the cave. I could feel the rocks beneath my hands and hear the faint sound of rushing water from somewhere.

Afraid to move and afraid to feel around, I frantically clicked my flashlight on and off. Nothing. I smacked the side of it against the palm of my hand and heard the sound of tinkling glass inside it.

The bulb had broken. My heart sank.

I couldn't hear anything from above. They must have *known* the rope broke and probably

79

ran to get another one. I would just wait right here until they found one. No big deal. I'd just wait right here. They'd be coming down soon.

Then I heard the shuffling noise.

I heard it even over the water and the noise in my head. I strained to see through the darkness. Just a wall of black. No light coming from anywhere!

I heard the shuffling noise again.

It hit me. The matches. USE THE MATCHES! I reached for my pocket and grabbed out the matches, fumbling with them.

Another shuffle.

My hands trembled. The box jerked open and the matches flew everywhere. In the dark. My heart sank lower.

I'd have to feel around for them. There was no other way. A dreadful tingle filled my body. I was breathing harder. It was hard to think straight. Little white dots exploded behind my eyes.

Another loud shuffle and a hollow thump, as if something big had hit a rock.

I jumped, startled.

I couldn't do it. I couldn't feel around with my hands in the pitch black dark. There could have been anything on the floor of this cave. Spiders. Snakes. Anything.

I felt stinging tears while I sat in the dark and waited.

Then another thought hit me. The camera. The camera had a flash. I could use the camera to see. If only for a moment. Long enough to find the matches. My face flushed and my heartbeat quickened.

I grabbed the camera and held it in front of me.

I hit the button.

POP! A loud pop and the cavern flooded with light! It was not as big as I thought it was. Slime and moss covered the walls. It looked like there might have been a crawl space to the right between some rocks.

"Aim at the ground next time, stupid," I said to myself as I aimed the camera at the ground and pressed the button.

Another POP and the cave floor lit up. I scanned as quickly as I could and saw a dozen matches out of the twenty in the box.

I felt a burst of relief. I felt around for the matches in the dark.

Another shuffle and a bump. I'd never be

able to sleep without a nightlight again.

It felt as if an hour had passed and I hadn't moved. Where were they?

I yelled for Billy and Erin. No answer. I felt sobs swell in my throat but I choked them down.

I lit match number fourteen in my fingers. When it would go out, I would light number fifteen out of the twenty.

If Erin and Billy were yelling for me, I couldn't hear them. Not over the water.

And not over the shuffling that grew louder and louder.

Match number sixteen.

Match number seventeen.

Match number eighteen. I tried my best to stay calm, to push back the feeling of panic. Surely Billy and Erin had gone to find another rope. My face was wet with smeared tears.

Match number nineteen. Had they forgotten me? Did they think I was dead? My mind had gone numb and I could hear myself breathe.

Match number twenty.

I screamed as loud as I possibly could. No response from above but it made me feel better to scream.

Still, I had to stay calm. I couldn't lose my head. I was out of matches and had about eight shots left on the camera. I couldn't *wait* to see this film developed. I'd look like the biggest rock fan of all time.

I tried to laugh, but the gnawing fear in my stomach wouldn't let me.

I inched my way in the dark over to where the crawl space opened in the side of the cave wall. I couldn't believe what I felt. A breeze!

The first nice thing I'd felt in this stupid hole. I suddenly felt my heart leap. I smiled despite myself.

This could lead to a way out!

I suspected a larger room might lie on the other side of the crawl space.

A larger room.

What the heck.

I carefully aimed the camera at the hole and pressed the button.

POP! There was *definitely* a larger room. I could see a much higher ceiling with huge stalactites and a sandy beach as well. It would be better than waiting for Erin and Billy in this cramped hole and I'd be only a few feet away.

I crawled through.

POP went the camera flash! I saw the crawl space get wider and wider until...

Blackness.

POP went the camera flash! I saw the room on the other side of it. An unbelievably beautiful cavernous room. Rocky cascades came down the walls in beautiful formations and stalactites hung low from the ceiling. Little hidden crawl spaces and shelves were everywhere.

Blackness.

POP went the camera flash! I saw black water rolling up onto the shore of the underground beach from the vast underground lake.

A secret lake far underground. All these years and no one knew about it.

Blackness.

I heard a loud shuffling, like a thousand pound sack dragging across the sand. Then a hissing noise. The kind of hissing that came from deep within the chest of something.

Something big.

POP went the camera flash! I looked to the left and saw a large brown, sack-like body covered in wrinkly skin.

POP! A snaky, muscular neck that

writhed high into the air.

POP! A hideous reptilian head, nasty black eyes and a vast jaw full of razor-like teeth.

POP! A head that bobbed a moment at the ceiling of the cave and then snaked down toward me.

Then darkness.

Nothing but darkness. The flash in the camera no longer worked. I could feel my heart jolt against my ribs. My mind raced in sheer, blinding terror as I tried to comprehend what I saw.

I could see nothing now.

But I could hear it.

I could hear the sound of wet, strained breathing coming toward me. Then I felt the breath hit my face, hot and sour. The monster's head hung inches in front of mine, swaying back and forth.

I could hear the awful beating of its huge heart and the shuffle of its flippers across the sand. I shared the same beach with the monster of Lake Wataga. A living, breathing relative of the plesiosaur, inches away from me.

I prayed that it wasn't hungry. My heart gave up hope in a scream. I could practically feel the jaws clamp around me tightly.

  Then I heard a terrific splash in the dark and I felt alone.

  Terribly alone.

18

I still stood there, frozen, staring at the water when the light came. A thin beam bounced over the blackness of the underground lake and then reflected off the sand. It finally came to rest on my face, temporarily blinding me.

"MICHELLE! Are you okay? We had to run all the way to Billy's house to get another rope. Michelle! What's wrong?" Erin shook me but I couldn't really hear her or feel her.

It took a moment to register what had happened. Finally my mind returned from the water. My eyes blinked as they adjusted to the light and filled with stinging tears.

"It was terrible! Oh, Erin, it was terrible!" I started to cry and it turned into sobbing and the sobbing into shrieking. The sounds of my scream echoed in the empty, prehistoric halls of this underground cave. I shook uncontrollably.

"Is she all right!?" Billy asked, shining the flashlight in all directions as if to ward off some attacking evil.

"I'm okay," I said, trembling and trying to get a grip on myself. "Just give me a minute." My self-control began to return.

"What is it? What happened?" Erin struggled to maintain control of her fear.

I just looked at her and tried to find words to describe what had happened. What I had seen.

My mind raced and I saw the flash of the camera in my head and saw the teeth, the face, that huge, horrid sack of a body. I couldn't describe it, but it didn't matter. I didn't have to.

"LOOK!" Billy cried, pointing to the shore with the flashlight.

Our eyes followed the beam to the sand. It looked as if a large bulldozer had plowed up the beach and then retreated. Clumps were still falling from the top of the pile of sand. It stood packed five feet high . . . and there were tracks.

Billy placed one foot in a diamond-shaped print, which dwarfed him. He could have laid down in it and still had room for a friend.

The sight left him almost speechless. "This thing is b-big," he stammered.

"You could say that," I laughed. My mind was ready to snap. I'd lose it for sure. It felt as if I had been up for days with no sleep. I had a horrible taste in my mouth and my stomach kept twitching. The monster. The claustrophobia. I knew I'd go insane if I didn't get out of that place immediately.

"You were right, Michelle! It must live down here. That's why it was never seen." Erin pointed out at the water. "Look at the size of this place. It's almost as big as the lake on the surface!"

"LOOK! Over there!" Billy swung the beam over to the shore near the opposite wall of the gigantic cave.

A rowboat sat on the shore, the water barely lapping against it.

The name on the side read:

"Gloucester II."

19

In the boat lay the mossy, weathered skeleton of Mr. Gloucester.

Half of the skeleton anyway.

I didn't want to think about what had happened to the other half.

A heavy canvas covered him, like an old yellowed sail. His arms had been placed neatly across his chest and two gold coins rested where his eyes used to be. An old fishing hat still sat on his bony head.

Against the boat leaned an old wooden plank with these words burned into it in epitaph:

"Here lies Harold P. Gloucester,
biologist, explorer and husband.
He found his monster at last.
And it found him."

We were stunned by the sight, unable to move or even breathe.

Billy whimpered and stepped backward, his eyes glued to the boat in disbelief.

I felt Erin trembling beside me.

"We've g-got to get out of here now," she stuttered.

I'd never seen a real skeleton before. I couldn't believe I was staring at human remains. I finally lost the weak hold on my panic.

As I turned to run, I saw a figure rise behind Billy.

I didn't have time to warn him.

He backed right into Mrs. Gloucester. The flashlight lit her ancient, withered face like a candle in a pumpkin as she clutched him around the chest with her bony arms.

20

"How did you find this hidden cavern? You must leave here at once! There's no telling when or if it will return!" Mrs. Gloucester cried as Billy pulled away. He practically fell into my arms.

Billy kept the light in her face as best he could, his grip on the flashlight so tight his knuckles turned white. The beam bounced around the cavern as he shook with fear.

Mrs. Gloucester lurched forward like a madwoman, hunched over like an animal with her teeth bared. "I've been trying to capture it for weeks! Now you're poking about where you don't belong. You've scared it away!"

She scanned the water frantically, her head jerking about. "Hurry! We haven't a second to spare!" she screeched, then raced down the beach toward an opening in the far wall of the cavern.

We followed without a sound. It was better than waiting around for that thing to come back.

The opening led to a natural rock staircase that led up into a dark passageway. Small yellow lights glowed from the walls at regular intervals. They seemed to be fiber optic strips, or like the lights on the floor of a movie theatre.

We paused to look at each other. Should we follow or should we stay here and wait for help? But who would show up? Who knew where we were? Of course we could go back the way we got in here in the first place. . .

"I'm going back to the rope!" Billy said reluctantly.

"And hope the thing won't pop up on the beach for a snack? I'm for following the crazy old woman," Erin said.

"Listen to what you just said! It's nuts!" Billy cried.

I remembered that thing's razor-sharp teeth and its glistening snake-like eyes.

A deafening roar shook the cavern.

"Let's go!" No one argued the point.

We ran into the passageway, leaping three rock steps at a time. We could barely make out the hunched figure that had paused about fifty feet ahead. A sickly yellow glow crept across her face from the lights in the walls.

"You're very lucky you're not resting in that thing's belly right now!" Gloucester snapped. "Hurry along! We've only a little further to go."

We followed as best we could but she easily outdistanced us. She darted around the rocks and under the overhangs as if she had done it a million times.

We went on for what seemed like miles, tripping and stumbling on loose rocks and sharp outcroppings. Gloucester never missed a beat.

"Hurry! We may still make it! We can beat it!" she cried.

I saw a faint blue light ahead and heard the sound of rushing water. It was an opening. An opening into a *larger* room in the cavern.

Gloucester stopped at the opening in the rock wall blocking the passage. A large waterfall fell in front of it, a breathtaking cascade.

The waterfall fell into the underground lake about fifty feet below. The ceiling of the cavern still towered above us.

We stepped forward and looked through the falling, sparkling water.

All around we saw dozens of little caverns and a honeycomb of openings sprinkled about the cave walls on the far shore of the underground lake.

Then we noticed the ski-lift chair.

It hung below the ledge where Mrs. Gloucester stood. Two adults could sit in it. . . or three of us.

A rope and pulley system suspended the chair and hung precariously across the wide chasm over the lake below.

I couldn't see any other way to get across.

We all looked at her as she gave the rope a couple of good tugs.

The chair bounced to and fro a moment, then stopped.

I had a very bad feeling about this.

Gloucester fixed her gaze on the underground lake below for a moment and seemed satisfied.

"I'll go first and send it back across. Do not question what I say. There is no time! I'll explain everything later. Hold on as tight as you can and don't let go, no matter what!"

Gloucester leaped into the chair and pressed a small button on the pole that jutted from the back. She didn't bother to sit down, simply crouched and clutched the pole. There was an electric whiff of ozone and a loud clanging grind as the chair moved forward, jerking toward the waterfall.

We crowded the opening as she passed *through* the waterfall and out, suspended over the lake.

I held my breath. She turned and looked back at us over her shoulder. She never took her eyes off us, no matter how hard the chair shook or the ropes pulled.

In a matter of seconds she climbed from the chair to the ledge above on the other side of the lake.

She pressed a button on the side of the wall and the chair moved back toward us, traveling backward even more erratically than it had moved before.

"I don't know if I can do this." Billy began to cry.

"I don't think we have a choice. There's no other way to go," I muttered, my gaze never leaving that wreck of a chair.

Erin took a deep breath and closed her eyes. "I'll get in first."

My mind went back to all the times we'd traveled to the snowy ski resort at the top of Big Bear Mountain.

I could see Erin and me waving to Mom and Dad. We would wait for the chair to approach the drop-off point, the ten minute ride up fueling our growing excitement. We'd be bundled tightly in our brightly colored ski jackets.

Bright smiles would fill our frostbitten faces as we'd prepare to jump off, clutching our poles and flexing our skis.

Erin would almost always fall out of the chair and smack her face right into the hard, frozen ground.

"I'll go first," I said.

She didn't argue.

The chair hit the ledge with a bouncing jolt and the electric motor hidden above kicked off.

I climbed in first and steadied the chair as best I could. Billy climbed in next.

"HURRY! HURRY!" Gloucester screamed to us. She jumped around, pointing at something below.

Something in the water.

I looked down and froze. I tried to cry out. To stop Erin from getting in the chair. To stop Billy from pressing the button on the pole.

Too late.

Erin sent the chair bouncing toward the waterfall with the weight of her leap as Billy pressed the button. It sent the motor into overload.

I saw bubbles fifty feet below on the lake's

surface. I saw a dark shadow swimming down the deep channel . . .

I saw the brown hump rise out of the water.

We hit the waterfall and the chair flew through, with a bounce of the rope, heading across the lake!

My scream carried us almost to the halfway point.

Billy clutched the center pole, his eyes clenched tight and his knuckles bone white.

Erin, off-balance, dropped into her seat. She screamed when she saw the monster below us.

From fifty feet above, we had a spectacular view, even through the murky water. The animal was shaped like a football with four flippers and a long rippling neck, capped with a huge snake-like head. It swam beneath us and doubled back. The reflections of the cavern played on its back as it dove straight down at an enormous speed.

We heard the sloshing of the displaced water. We heard the crashing of six foot waves against the rocky walls. We saw the graceful neck arching back, as if in preparation to...

Could a plesiosaur jump?

We couldn't do anything but sit in the chair like three worms on a hook. Nowhere to run. Nowhere to hide. Not even a rock to throw at it.

"Mrs. Gloucester!" I yelled.

"HOLD ON!" we heard her call from the opposite ledge.

A brief moment of silence. The chair sputtered, putted forward. We looked briefly and longingly at the safety of the opposite ledge a million miles away. Then we looked back down.

A geyser of mammoth proportions erupted from the lake below. It was both real and unreal. A large dark shadow exploded from the center of the water.

A mouth!

The mouth, large as a cave and filled with razor-sharp teeth, hurtled straight up at us! Two black eyes glistened from the sides of this mouth, and a vast body trailed behind it. A hurricane of hot, foul breath blew our hair straight back.

It had jumped!

Instinctively we all pulled our feet up, screaming. The mouth of this mammoth head snapped shut about two inches below the bottom of the chair.

It seemed to hang in the air below our chair for a long moment . . . suspended there. The body fell back first, pulling the neck and head down with it. The resulting splash sent our transport rocketing into the ledge on the other side.

Erin fell out of the chair.

Billy grabbed her, then clutched at me.

Gloucester dragged us all onto the ledge with a super-human burst of strength.

"If we hurry, we can still trap it," Mrs. Gloucester growled.

We ran down and down and down, over boulders and past sharp rocky corners. Down the rough hewn rocks we flew.

Gloucester led the way, traversing the path as if being in the cave made her feel young again, as if she were alive as she hadn't been before, with a madness in her eyes.

She was a woman as possessed as her husband before her must have been.

"He's still in the cavern, lucky for you," she growled.

"You lured it down here with the decoy monster, right?" Billy asked breathlessly, struggling to keep up.

"After two weeks of trying. I can't bait it as well as Harold could. By the way, his name is Wattie. Harold named him." Gloucester turned a corner.

"Mr. Gloucester caught . . . Wattie?" I asked.

"Yes. And Wattie caught him. Half of him anyway. Over forty years ago. He's only escaped from the cavern to the above ground lake twice since then. You were there the second time," she said angrily.

"Yesterday morning?"

"Yes. He sensed your movements in the water and came to investigate . . . and to feed. Lucky for you he prefers large schools of fish."

Gloucester reached the end of the hallway. She hesitated at a fork in the passage. To the right, a large ramp led to a dim, but wonderful shaft of light about three hundred yards ahead. To the left, a passageway led straight down to darkness.

She took the left fork in the darkness.

We followed. She obviously knew the caverns better than we did.

"Harold decided to keep Wattie a secret

and study him in private. He planned to stun the world with his discovery, but only when the right time came. He built all these contraptions and passages over the years."

"How did you keep it down here?" Billy asked, panting for breath.

"Aha!" Gloucester cried.

We reached another shore of the underground lake, where a large outlet flowed in two directions, like a broad underground river. One passage led to the left, one passage to the right.

Gloucester didn't waste any time. She ran to a large-yellow rubber raft on the sandy shore. She quickly shoved it across the sand, signaling to us for help.

We helped push the raft, loaded with electronic tracking equipment, into the water.

"We built a large steel gate that seals off both ends of this inlet. This is where it leaves this secret cavern to get to the above ground lake, and this is where we can trap it."

The raft bobbed on the water and she signaled for us to get in, quickly.

I went first, then Billy, then Erin. Gloucester stayed in the water, pushing the boat out toward the center of the river, in waist-deep water. Her shirt tails floated on top of the murky water like seaweed.

"This raft will take you around that corner and to a beach. You'll see the way out then. Go and don't look back."

"What about you!" Billy cried, standing up with unsteady legs. The boat tipped and threatened to capsize.

"SIT DOWN YOUNG MAN! I can handle everything from here. You just be sure to take that left fork. Understand? If you take the right fork, YOU WILL DIE! Do you understand?! TAKE THE LEFT FORK!" She stared at me as the raft drifted toward the split in the underground river. I nodded.

Erin grabbed a paddle from the floor of the raft and held it like a club.

The crashing wave of the river attacked the wall of rock between the two passages of the underground river. Left or right. We had to choose. Quickly.

To the right, the water roared down a dark tunnel at a terrific rate of speed. It seemed to plunge down into some kind of rapids. I could see the white caps and hear the thunder of water over rocks.

"Okay," I said.

The tunnel to the left looked darker and nastier. The water flow seemed to stay the same. Not as fast and a lot smoother. . . but darker, a lot darker.

"All right," I said. "Either way we go, we're dead."

"What do you mean? The crazy old woman said go to the left! So let's go to the left!" Billy grabbed for the paddle, but Erin threatened to hit him with it.

The raft continued to drift toward the wall, at which point we wouldn't have to make a decision. The river would do it for us.

"She got us this far, Michelle," Erin said. "If she wanted the plesiosaur to get us, she would have let it get us on the beach. Why would she lead us all the way here, if she wanted us to be monster chow? She seemed awfully worried when we were on the chairlift, too."

Erin started paddling hard to the left. I started to help, but when I looked down into that murky black water, I had second thoughts.

"GO! ERIN! GO!" Billy yelled.

With Erin's help, the raft hit a natural current that swept us toward the left tunnel.

Faster and faster. Soon Erin didn't have to paddle at all.

The opening of the left tunnel loomed before us. The little natural light which filtered into the cavern didn't exist in the tunnel. Only black, pitch dark in there.

I felt a sudden swell of alarm.

It was so powerful, I had to stand up, almost knocking Billy overboard.

"We messed up! We shouldn't have listened to her!" A sense of dread consumed me. The mouth of that tunnel loomed closer and with each stroke of the paddle I knew we were sailing straight to our doom.

"You decide that now?" Billy screamed.

"It's too late! Hang on!" Erin cried.

We hit the tunnel and plunged.

Down, down, down, through absolute darkness we plunged.

During the nearly vertical fall, I felt myself leave the raft several times before the sudden, violent jolt and tremendous splash at the bottom. My stomach and heart met somewhere in my chest.

Darkness and silence.

"Is everyone all right?" I asked groggily.

"Yeah." Erin was on the floor of the raft about two feet behind me. She'd been in front of me *before* the fall.

"Billy?"

No reply.

"BILLY?" I called again.

"BILLY!" I screamed for him now. I desperately felt around the raft for him, groping blindly. No Billy. My mind raced. Billy was gone. All my fault. I felt my stomach fly into my throat.

I listened carefully. I had taken a deep breath in preparation for another yell when I heard a noise. It came from behind. A small feeble cry for help, choked out by spurts and spits of water.

Billy. In the water behind us, judging from the sound.

Then the lights came on.

I heard a series of loud SNAPS! and bright floodlights filled our eyes.

The light blinded me at first, but when my eyes adjusted, I saw that we were in a narrow tunnel, about ten feet across, with slow flowing water that ended in a large steel grate about fifty feet ahead! The water would continue to flow through, but we sure wouldn't!

The lights shone down on us from about ten feet up, near the ceiling of the tunnel.

"She lied to us," I muttered.

Erin and I looked behind us.

Billy, wide-eyed and pale as a sheet, frantically swam toward the raft, spitting out water. Behind him I saw the ten foot waterfall that had tossed us out into this dead-end tunnel.

I don't know why he hurried to reach the raft. We were all trapped.

No way out.

22

The sound of evil laughter filled the tunnel. It sounded as if it came from some kind of speaker system in the walls! A woman's laughter.

Rock panels slid up on the left side of the tunnel, revealing a wall of thick plexi-glass. Steel beams in two layers reinforced it, obviously to withstand some serious impacts from something . . . large.

Behind the glass in a small, makeshift control room stood Mrs. Gloucester. Her eyes glowed with insanity as she paced among the wreckage of an electronics disaster.

It looked as if a fire had swept through the control room previously and she had tried to put it back together. A charred black chair lay overturned behind her in a pile of burned books. Blackened control panels behind her spewed showers of sparks.

With each crackle and snap from the control room, the lights would blink off . . . and then on, erratically, threatening to go out altogether.

Gloucester stepped forward to the glass and pressed her wrinkled face flat against it. She blew hard against the glass and her cheeks inflated like balloons. She broke out laughing again.

"Come on now! You'll have to make more noise than that!" she crowed over the speakers.

"LET US OUT OF HERE!" I yelled angrily, smacking the glass hard with my fists. The boat had drifted close to the glass and we could look straight into the crazed, laughing face of Mrs. Gloucester. The water came halfway up the glass wall.

I darted to the back of the raft to grab Billy out of the water. He had almost reached us and seemed to be saying something through the gulps and splashes of water.

"After the electrical fire, Harold got very upset. You see, the controls went out and we . . . lost him . . . Wattie I mean, not Harold." Gloucester seemed to be talking to herself more than to us.

Billy had almost made it to the raft.

"Come on, Billy," I yelled. "You can make it!"

Erin stared into Gloucester's face, entranced by her story. The old woman's raspy voice continued the tale.

"We could have been the most famous monster-hunters in the world! Think of it. A live Plesiosaur! The stuff of legends! And it was *ours. OURS!*

"Imagine that you'd found the most precious pet in all the world and you loved it more than anything, more than your own life. It was something you'd waited your entire life to find. Something so much more important than yourself, you could never even *hope* to see it, let alone find it. *Capture it .We did. We captured a dream. The dream of a lifetime.*

"Now imagine how you'd feel about someone taking it *away* from you and you being powerless to stop it.

"We could not allow this to happen. Why should *we* share our discovery with people who would mistreat it? A bizarre curiosity to be marveled at for a few moments and then forgotten.

"Headline news for a day. What then? No

one would care for it, not the way we did. No one to love it, not the way we did. Just a headline for a day.

"Harold was furious. Livid. Mad enough to . . .Well, it was all *my* fault, you understand. I thought I'd fixed those gate controls. I was SURE OF IT!"

I locked onto Billy's hand.

He looked at me with an expression that I will remember for the rest of my life.

"It's coming right behind me," he gasped.

A blackness at the mouth of the tunnel filled it completely.

We heard a strange *whoomping* sound. Like something had been plugged into a drain, now becoming unplugged.

Then we saw *the hump* pushing through the water straight toward us.

It approached rapidly, with a purpose in its movement now. It knew this place and it knew what it wanted.

We looked from the hump back to Gloucester, tapping her finger on the glass.

"Harold was where you are now, splashing about and screaming to attract Wattie's attention. You see, he wouldn't fall for the rubber decoy anymore. He'd learned to tell the difference between something alive and something *not alive*.

"So Harold played the role of live bait and it worked. Wattie came for him. He came for him the way he comes for you now. . ."

A sudden choking gulp and Gloucester screamed, her mouth thrown wide in a terrifying wail of grief and sorrow.

She regained control enough to grab a handle on the panel in front of her.

"I promised I'd make it up to him. I swore I'd catch it again. *And I did. . .*"

Gloucester howled with delight!

She pulled the lever.

23

"I HAVE HIM NOW! AT LAST!" Gloucester screamed. A loud clanging echoed behind the walls. A shiny new steel gate started to close at the mouth of the tunnel at the waterfall that had dropped us here.

The gate strained against the water and the rocks and the backwash of a powerful tail.

It closed behind the hump swimming toward us, sealing it off, sealing us in with it.

I hauled Billy into the raft.

"We have to get out of here! NOW!" I yelled, as his weight threw us both into the floor.

Mrs. Gloucester pressed her face against the glass wall and followed the creature's every move.

She watched every movement of the creature, every stroke and every twitch of its brown, slug-like form.

A rough flipper squeaked as it rubbed against the glass, smearing it with a film of slime. This seemed to delight Gloucester. Her hands raised into the air as if she had just scored the winning touchdown in the playoffs.

"You are mine!"

We stared down the tunnel in terrified silence, the turbulence of the water the only movement.

With a small splash, a snaky head rose from the water. Its mouth opened like a steel trap and it emitted a dreadful hissing.

"THE GRATE! IT'S OUR ONLY CHANCE!" I yelled. "NOW!"

The three of us dove into the water, kicking the raft into the gaping jaws behind us.

We swam frantically for the grate blocking the other end of the tunnel, the black water nearly impossible to see through.

The huge beast's horrid teeth sank into the yellow raft, slicing it to ribbons with a loud POP!

We could see nothing underwater but we could feel the rough, sharp edges of the holes in the grate. Holes too small for an adult to pass through . . . but we could.

We wiggled through them to the other side, away from the Plesiosaur.

Our heads shot out of the water.

The water on this side of the grate was much shallower and we could actually stand up.

"LOOK OUT!" I screamed, grabbing Billy by the shirt.

I pulled him away from the grate just as a large snaky head slammed into it, its jaws wide and its breath like a wind-tunnel.

The teeth in those chomping jaws were as long as my forearm. It snarled and snapped but couldn't fit its head through the grate.

I breathed in relief. Then it reared back its head and SMASHED into the grate again.

I watched bits of rock tumble from around the steel grate's frame and my heart leaped in my chest. I screamed.

The rock around the grate began to give way. IT WAS BREAKING THROUGH!

Large chunks of rock fell from the ceiling into the water as we splashed in a panic through the water, running down the tunnel.

The long neck unfurled behind us, its

head twitching and turning and completely filling the passage. It was coming after us, smashing and widening the crumbling passage as it came.

Could we outrun it?

The water became more shallow as we followed the passage up a ramp.

It soon led us into the hallway where we had been before!

We stood before the split in the tunnel. The one leading to the chairlift and one leading to the beautiful shaft of light! We had made a big circle!

"Oh great!" Billy cried. "She's gonna figure out what happened to us any minute. No telling where she'll pop out. We're dead. We're monster chow."

"Come on. We'll go to the right," I gasped. "She lied to us before. It's probably the way out." We stood bent over, trying to catch our breath. Holding onto our knees, we sucked in large gulps of musty cavern air. We were so exhausted, our knees trembled and our legs seemed to be made of lead.

Erin suddenly looked up in alarm. "Listen. Do you hear it?"

The sound of crashing rock and breaking glass. A horrible noise like a bomb going off.

A woman's scream.

We looked at each other.

A horrid cry shook the wall of the cavern.

A loud scraping noise came from the passage behind us.

"Did you hear it?" Billy asked.

We nodded.

The noise came from the passage again. A familiar sound by now, like a thousand pound sack of sand dragging itself across the rocks. In my mind, I saw the Plesiosaur on the beach, felt paralyzing fear and watched as it reared its snaky head back to strike!

We ran into the right passage, screaming! The yellow lights on the wall were only blurs as we sped past them.

"HURRY!" I yelled. Tears ran down my face.

The sound came closer.

We ran to the end of the passage, feeling the cool rock walls with our trembling hands.

We could see an opening to a starry sky and a bright moon overhead.

A narrow stone staircase had been carved

into the wall that wound in a spiral up to the opening.

We stumbled up the stairway, hearing the rocks crumble and collapse behind us.

In the cave below, a large shadow crawled across the ground.

One, two, three. We popped into the fresh night air. We had emerged from the well in Gloucester's backyard!

We scrambled across the grass, tumbled into a heap and stared back at the well. Our limbs collapsed from exhaustion and our heads went light in relief.

Suddenly a strong, flexible neck unfurled from the well. A snake-like head reared against the starry sky and let out a startling cry, its eyes as bright as any of the stars above it.

What a breathtaking sight. Just for an instant that monster was *absolutely beautiful*.

The most beautiful thing in the world.

I understood then, what Gloucester saw in the monster of Lake Wataga. Beauty. Sheer majesty. It glistened in the moonlight like something that didn't belong to this world.

Like it was somehow above it all.

More important, I knew what she meant.

I too felt a desire to keep it to myself.

To keep the secret.

The slit-like eyes rolled and its massive head vanished back down into the well.

As if it had never been there.

We lay on the grass for the rest of the night, staring at the well.

And remembering.

The next day, it took nearly five hours to explain our absence to Mom and Dad. We didn't tell them about Wattie or about Mrs. Gloucester. Only that we had explored The Hole and got lost.

Mom and Dad were furious, issuing punishments, quick and severe. But I could tell they were really relieved that we were okay.

Later that afternoon, some reporters asked to interview Dad on the lake shore, near the spot where we saw the monster the first time. After the interview, they would air Dad's videotape.

It was an event unprecedented in the history of the lake.

All the residents of Lake Wataga came to share the excitement. The people of Fairfield who spent their summers in neat little cabins on this now famous lake came to the shore as well.

Doug Farner's souvenir stand was crowded to capacity and amateur monster watchers occupied every inch of sand.

Boats readied their sonars. A minisubmarine received its last minute checks. Men and women in lab coats tested and retested underwater cameras and strobes before lowering them into the murky, brown waters.

On the lake shore stood the sheriff, my father, and me. The camera lights kicked on and the noise from the newsvan crackled and sputtered as this live feed went to TV sets all over the country.

"So, how did it feel, little lady? To be chased by a legendary lake monster?" The reporter held the microphone in front of me. I saw Mom waving from behind the cameraman, looking flushed and excited.

"Not that bad," I said into the microphone.

This seemed to amuse the reporter.

"You weren't scared? Not many people get so close to something so unusual. Some people almost envy you!" he smiled.

The reporter shifted his attention to Dad. "Where did you first see the monster?"

Dad was about to answer when George Myer pointed toward the middle of the lake.

"THERE IT IS!" he cried. "THE MONSTER!"

There off the shore about two hundred yards away, a brown hump broke the surface of the water.

It turned to face the camera and moved faster, leaving behind a "V" shaped wake.

It was almost popping a wheelie.

"Billy's such a show off," I whispered to Erin.

"I-t-t's coming straight for us!" Mrs. Myer stammered. The camera had swung, under the reporter's insistence, to the lake.

The people backed up slowly and all eyes were on the water.

Except for mine. I slipped through the crowd to walk back to the house.

"It's incredible, ladies and gentlemen. We are seeing live the incredible monster of Lake Wataga. It appears to be about thirty or so feet long, brown and wrinkled and swimming straight toward us. It's almost to the shore . . .

it's . . . it's . . ."

The sheriff carefully bent over and grabbed the back of the "monster" as it beached itself with a soft slush of sand. He and Dad hauled it the rest of the way.

It dropped with the unmistakable sigh of air escaping. A big, brown, rubber sack with a square engine poking out of its deflating back.

"It's a hoax!" the reporter concluded into the microphone. "A cleverly built hoax."

A moan rose from the crowd that immediately began to disperse. Some of the curious pushed closer to see.

"NO! NO!" cried Doug Farner as he clutched at the brown rubber thing with tears in his eyes. His arms embraced it, as if trying to get it to inflate again and somehow bring the legend back to life.

There was a loud POP! as the newspaper reporter's cameras went off.

A picture of Doug Farner, his face sorrowful as he held the Lake Wataga Hoax, graced the front page of newspapers across the country.

There is a special radio control device that sits in a place of honor in Billy Keen's room. It's the only clean spot *in* his room. He doesn't use it for anything anymore and he won't tell you what it's for, even if you ask him.

"It's just a trophy," he'll say.

A trophy well earned.

Erin and I often lie on the daybed in the picture window of our cabin, staring at the twinkling lake that glows so brilliantly in the moonlight.

Often, when it's quiet and calm, we see a swan-like neck rise from the water and the most carefully guarded secret of Lake Wataga will take a moonlight swim.

About the Authors

Marty M. Engle and **Johnny Ray Barnes Jr.**, graduates of the Art Institute of Atlanta, are the creators, writers, designers and illustrators of the **Strange Matter**™ series and the **Strange Matter**™ World Wide Web page.

Their interests and expertise range from state of the art 3-D computer graphics and interactive multi-media, to books and scripts (television and motion picture).

Marty lives in La Jolla, California with his wife Jana and twin terror pets, Polly and Oreo.

Johnny Ray lives in Tierrasanta, California and spends his free time with his fiancée, Meredith.

And now
an exciting preview
of the next

#6 Bad Circuits
by Johnny Ray Barnes, Jr.

A strange noise came from Daniel's room. That's not unusual. He's always working on some great secret, but he was never this loud about it before.

"Stephanie, could you go up there and see what, exactly, Daniel is doing?" Aunt Gail asked.

"Certainly." I finished my glass of water and trotted up the stairs.

Daniel didn't answer the first time I knocked, so I added more force to my next rap, and the one after that, and the one after that.

Finally, he came to the door. "Uh, yeah?" he asked, cracking the door just enough so I could see that he had his goggles on. He always wore them for working on electronic circuits.

"Aunt Gail wants to know what you're doing," I told him. He leaned his head out further to see if Aunt Gail had followed me.

"Stephanie, what I'm doing right now, it's nothing bad. You can tell her that." He grinned.

"She's going to want to know more than that." I pushed the door open to enter his room.

"Okay, okay, okay. But you have to keep it a secret." Daniel spoke softer, as if bargaining.

Until that point, Daniel and I had never shared a secret. I nodded.

"All right." He sighed in relief. "But first I have to set it up, so turn around and I'll tell you when you can look."

I turned my back, and waited impatiently as Daniel rummaged around, apparently trying to find everything he needed to put together his secret.

"Okay, Steph, turn around."

When I turned, I saw Daniel had placed an egg-shaped box made out of green and black circuit boards on his desk.

"What is it? A sculpture?" I asked.

He frowned.

"This is no sculpture. Sculptures don't think. They don't answer questions you ask them, at least not in the literal sense. They don't learn," Daniel retorted. He picked up the egg and brought it over to me. "But this soon will. Stephanie, this is an Electronic Brain."

I took it gingerly, and looked it over. An egg, made of bits of circuit boards taken from who knows what, and stuffed with computer memory chips and a bundle of wires.

"See that light on the top?" he asked.

I saw a little red bulb.

"When that bulb's on, the brain is thinking."

"What's it thinking?" I handed the egg back.

"Well, let's see." Daniel took one end of a cord already hooked into the computer on his desk, and plugged the free end into the Electronic Brain. He switched on the computer.

Nothing happened.

Suddenly, the red bulb came on, and numbers began to fill the screen, scrolling continuously. First zeros and ones, then a jumble of digits, completely random.

"That's just what I thought." Daniel tapped the screen with his finger.

"What's it mean?"

"The brain hasn't learned our language yet. It's trying to communicate with the only thing it knows, numbers."

"What're you going to do with it?" I asked.

"Well, first, I'm going to teach it how to speak. It has to learn to communicate using our language. Then, I'm going to enter it as my exhibit in the Fairfield Junior Science Competition. The Electronic Brain's going to help me beat out Frank Dunk for the first time in four years. The first prize is mine." He turned off the Brain, grinning from ear to ear.

Obviously he saw his triumph as clearly as the numbers flowing up the screen.

"Daniel, look!" I pointed at the Brain.

The red light on top was still glowing.

"What's it doing, Daniel?" I asked.

Daniel peered at it intently.

"Wow," he said. "It's thinking. It's thinking all by itself."